BIG BANG!
DUST CLOUDS, ENERGY AND THE UNIVERSE
COSMOLOGY FOR KIDS
CHILDREN'S COSMOLOGY BOOKS

PROFESSOR GUSTO
EDUCATIONAL & INFORMATIVE BOOKS FOR CHILDREN
(PRE-K / K-12)

All Rights reserved. No part of this book may be reproduced or used in any way or form or by any means whether electronic or mechanical, this means that you cannot record or photocopy any material ideas or tips that are provided in this book

Copyright 2016

Look at the stars in the sky.
Aren't they beautiful?
How did they get there?
How did they come to be?

How did the universe come into existence?

Our galaxy is just a small part of the vast universe. Every planet has its own number of moons and stars, asteroids and meteors.

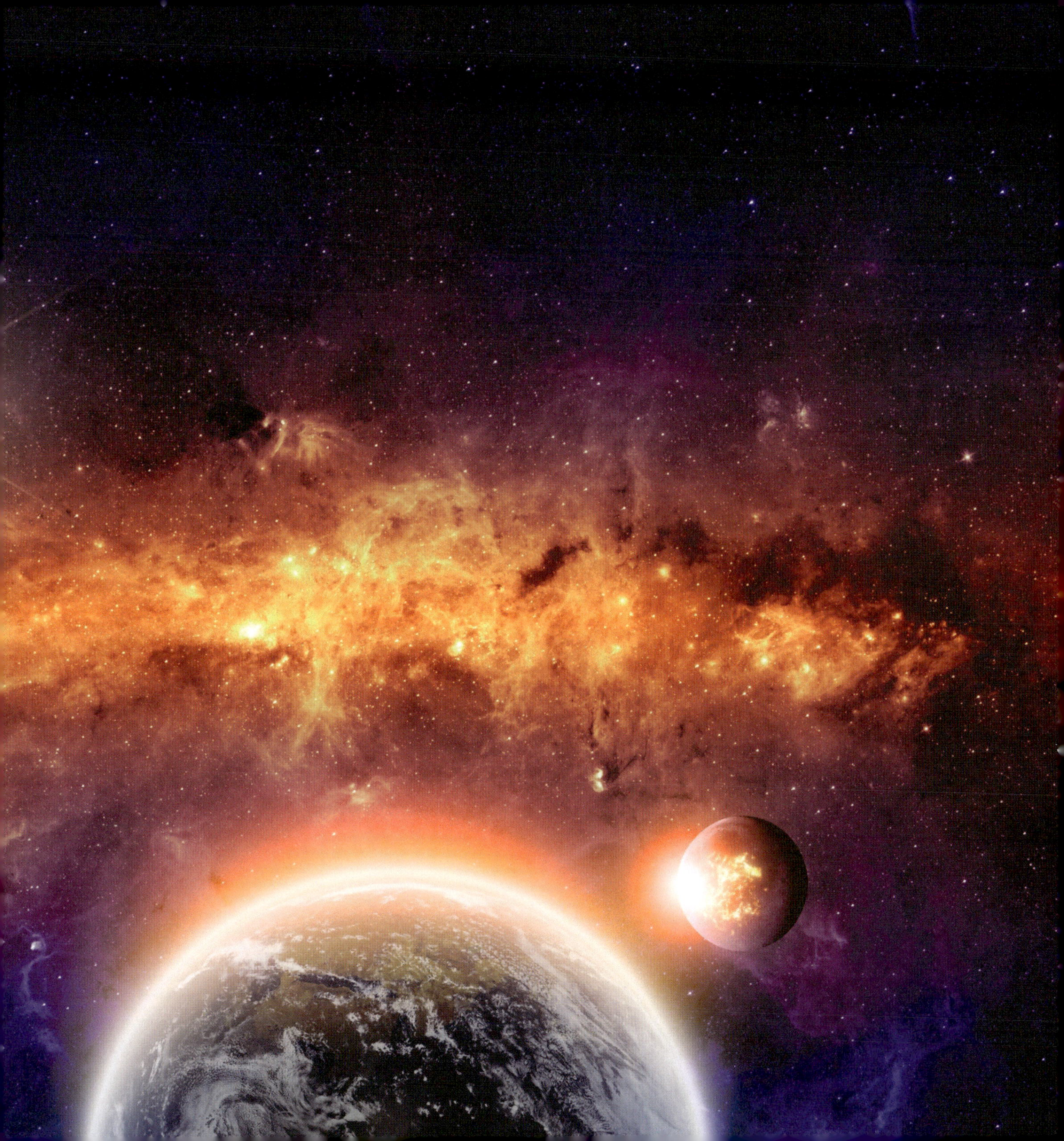

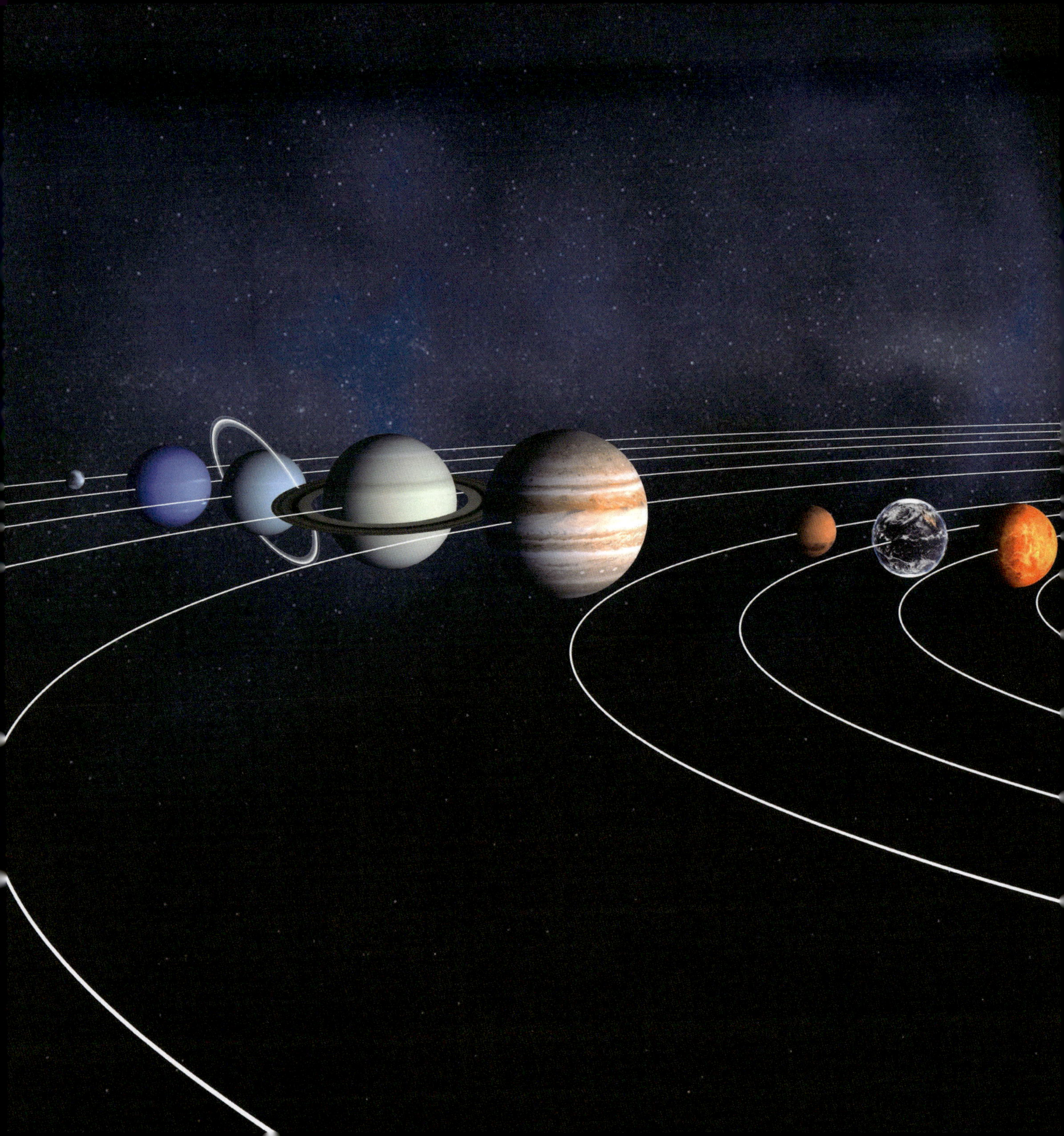

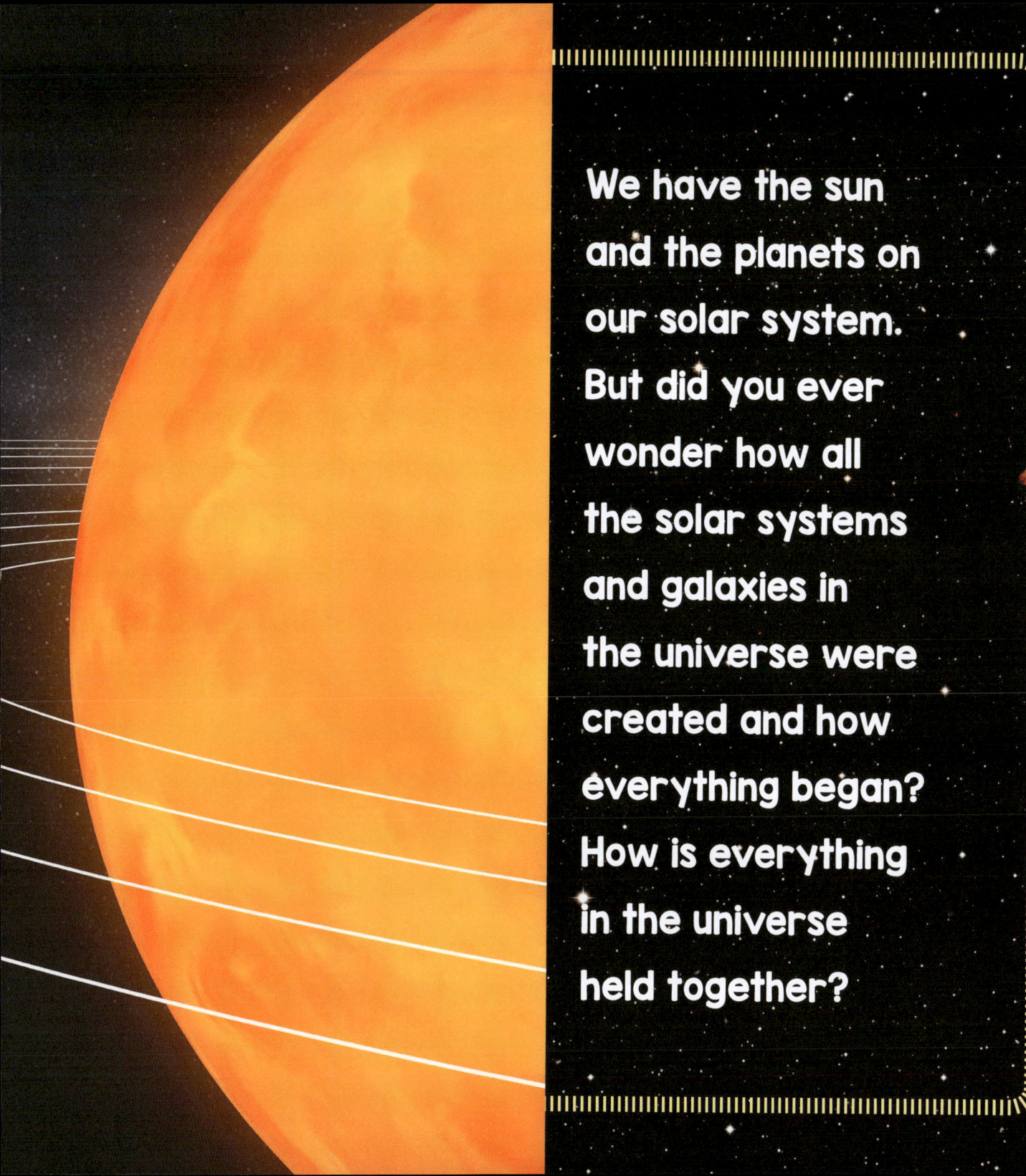

We have the sun and the planets on our solar system. But did you ever wonder how all the solar systems and galaxies in the universe were created and how everything began? How is everything in the universe held together?

What is the Big Bang Theory?

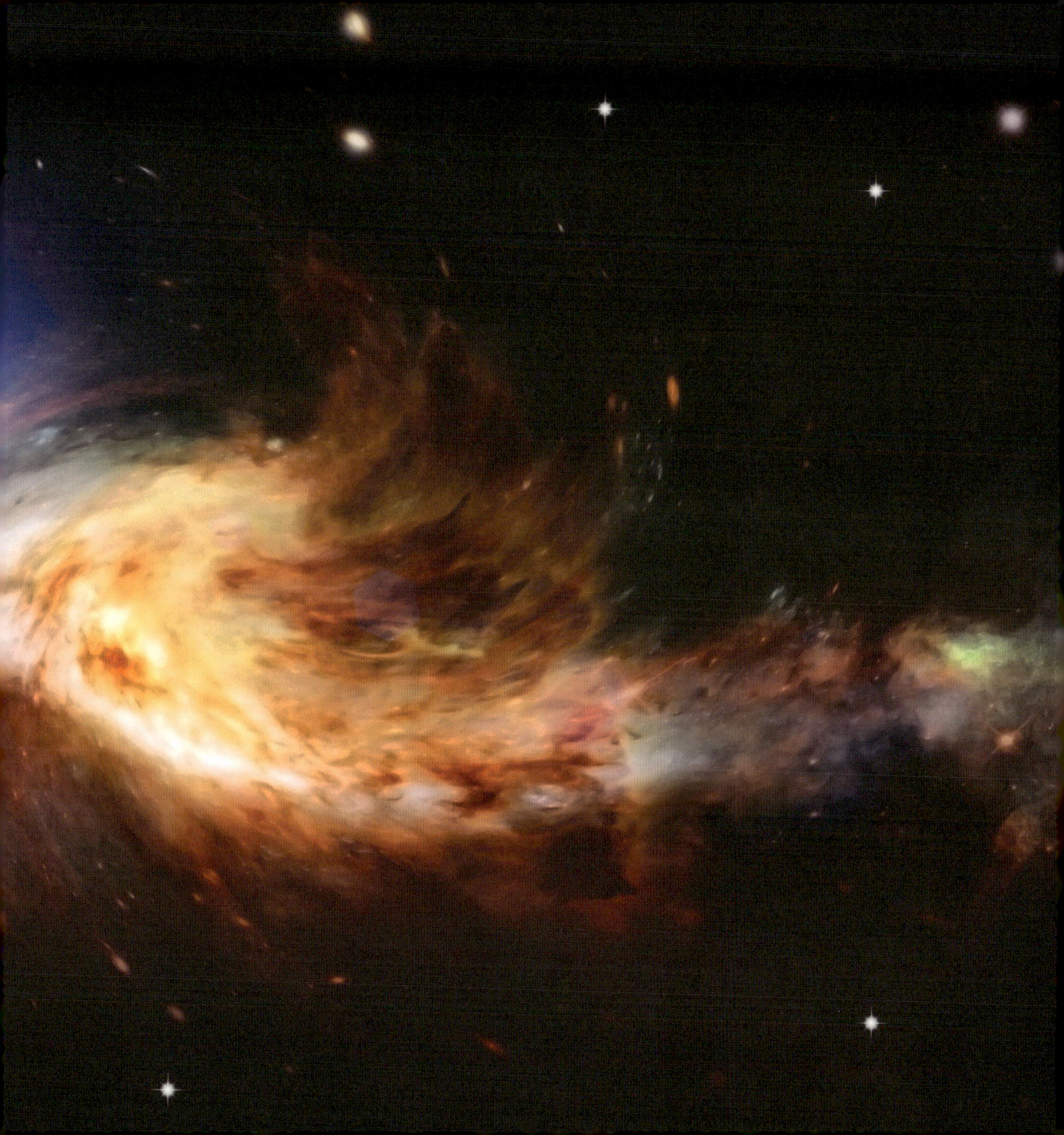

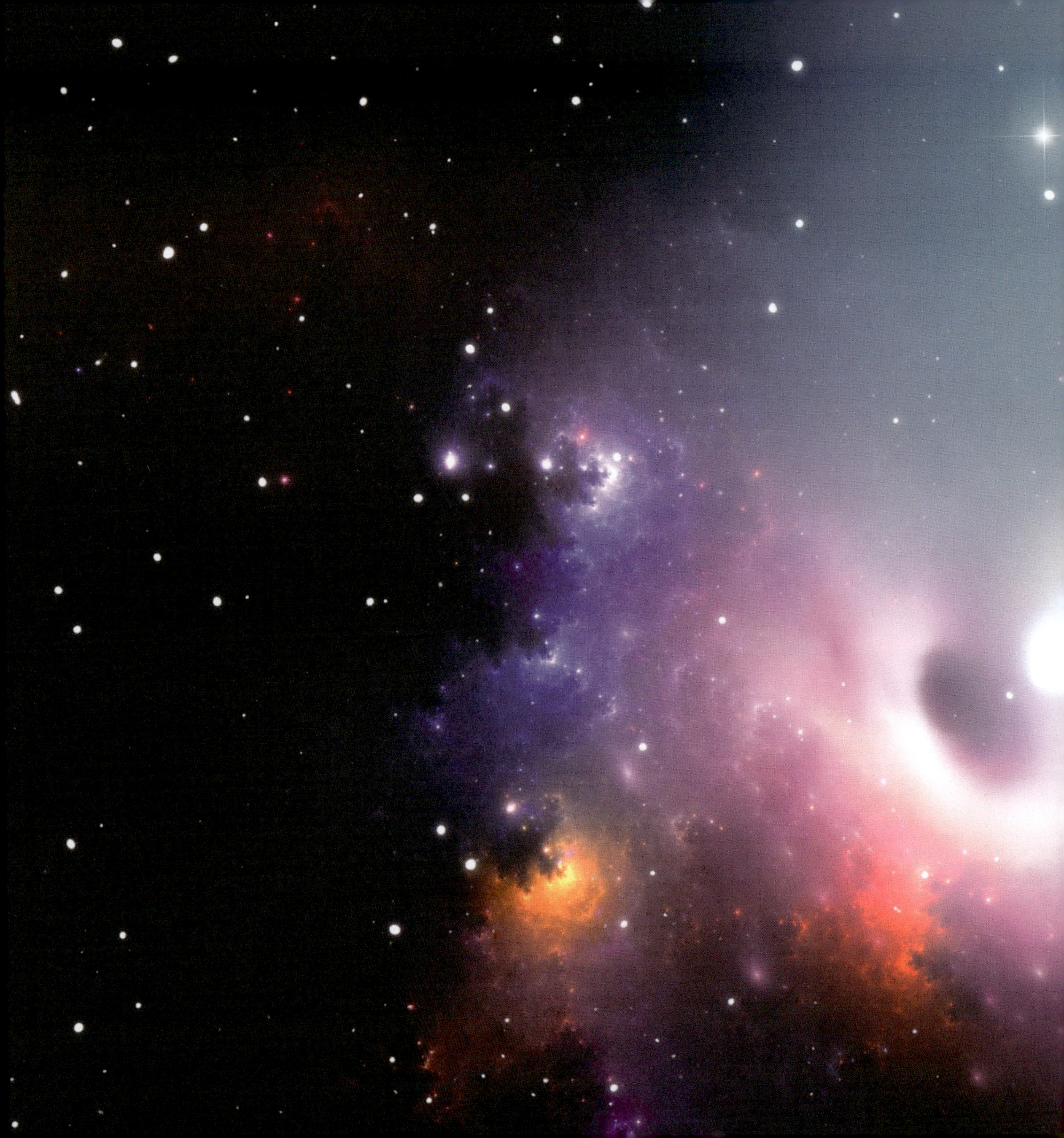

The origin of the galaxies, planets, stars, the sun and the universe as a whole is explained by the Big Bang Theory. According to the theory, the Big Bang happened 13.73 billion years ago and that it was the very beginning of the creation of the universe.

It all began with nothing. There was no space, no matter, no energy or time. A very tiny, hot point was all there was. It consisted of matter. It is believed that the point contained the whole universe!

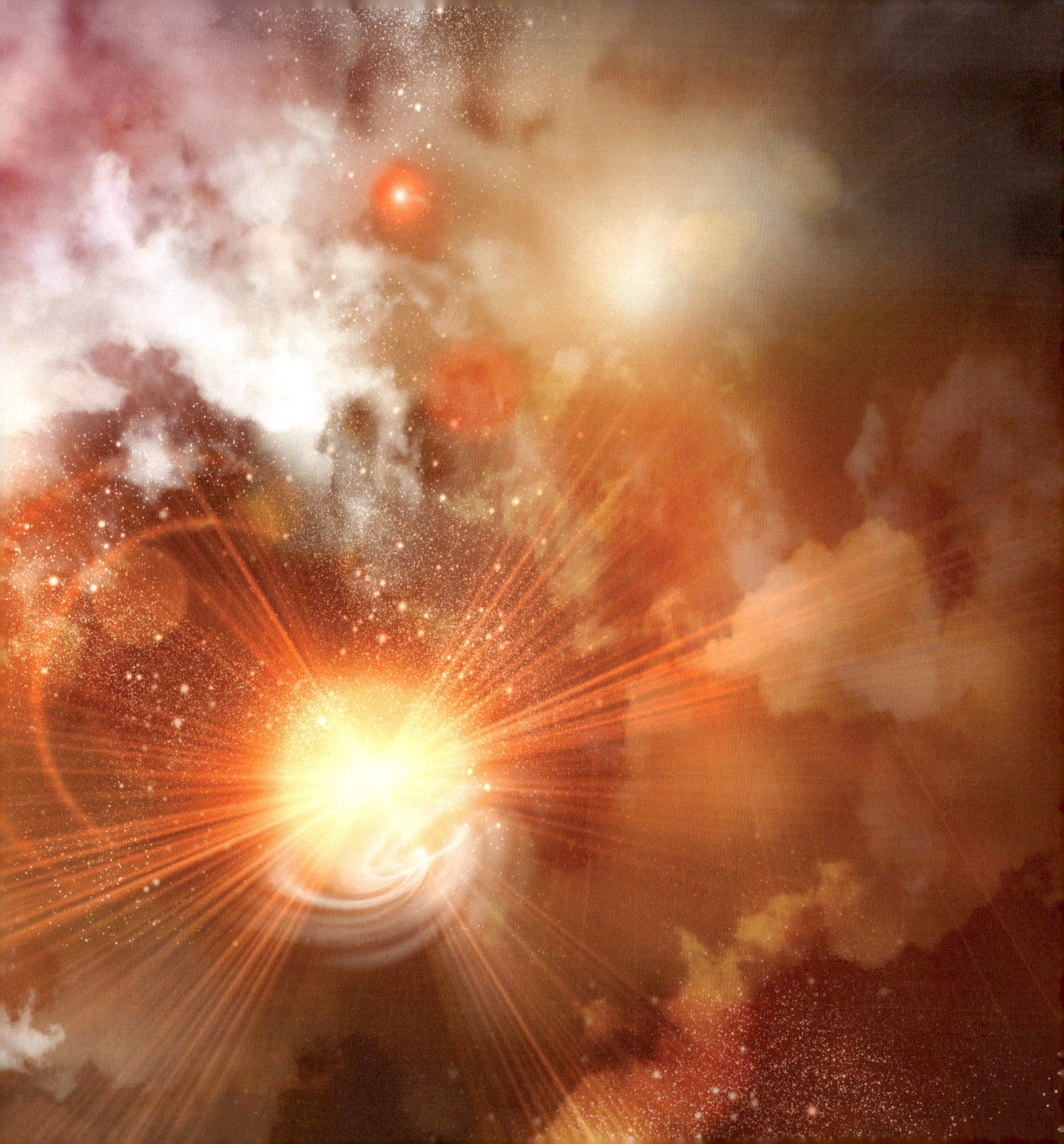

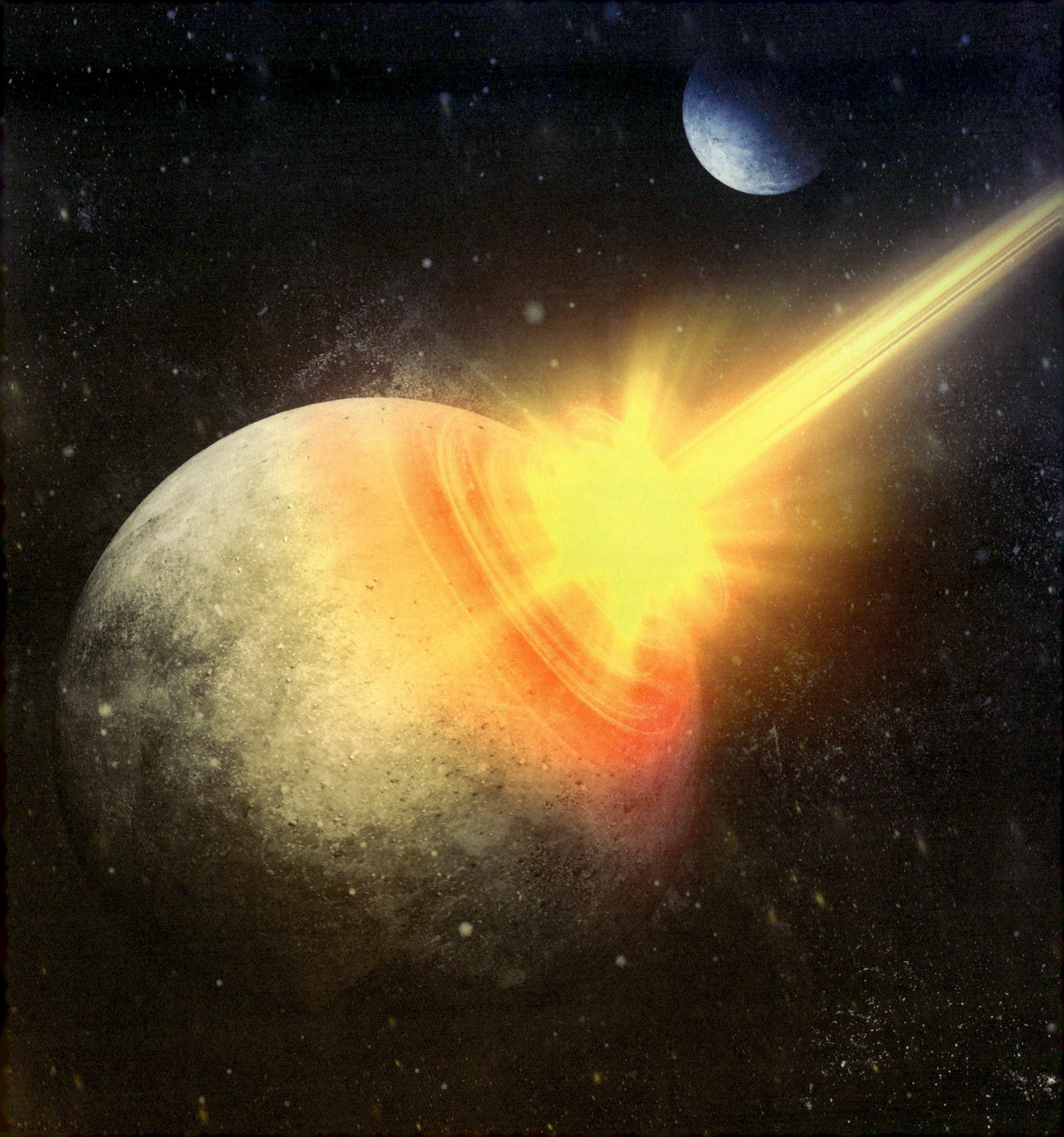

That very tiny point exploded! What did it become? That bang was the creation of the universe. At that point, time, space and energy were created. As soon as the very hot point burst, atoms began to form.

Galaxies began to form after a period of time. Planets began to form after some billions of years. Then, the most exciting part of creation began. Life began to form on Earth after some millions of years.

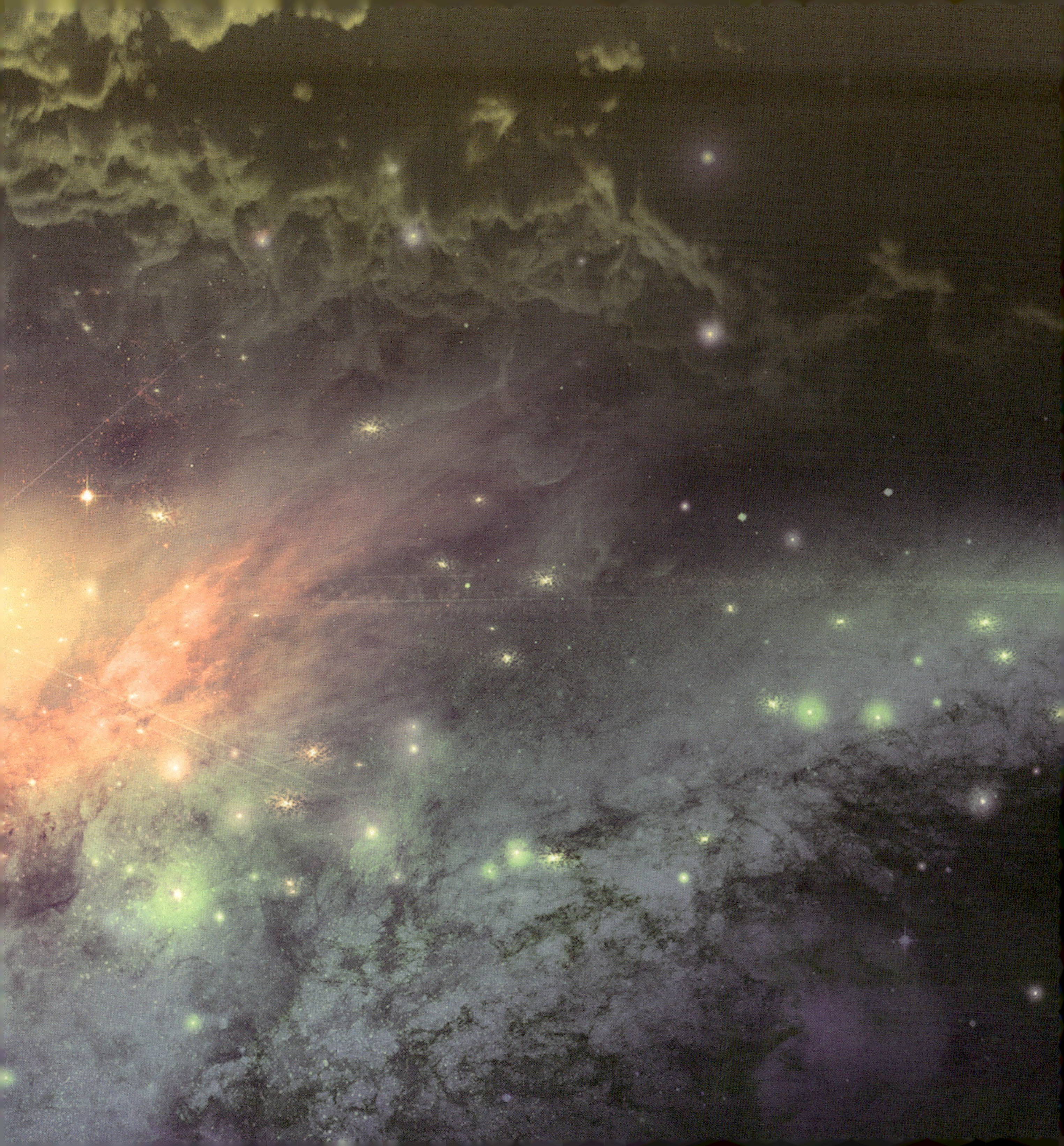

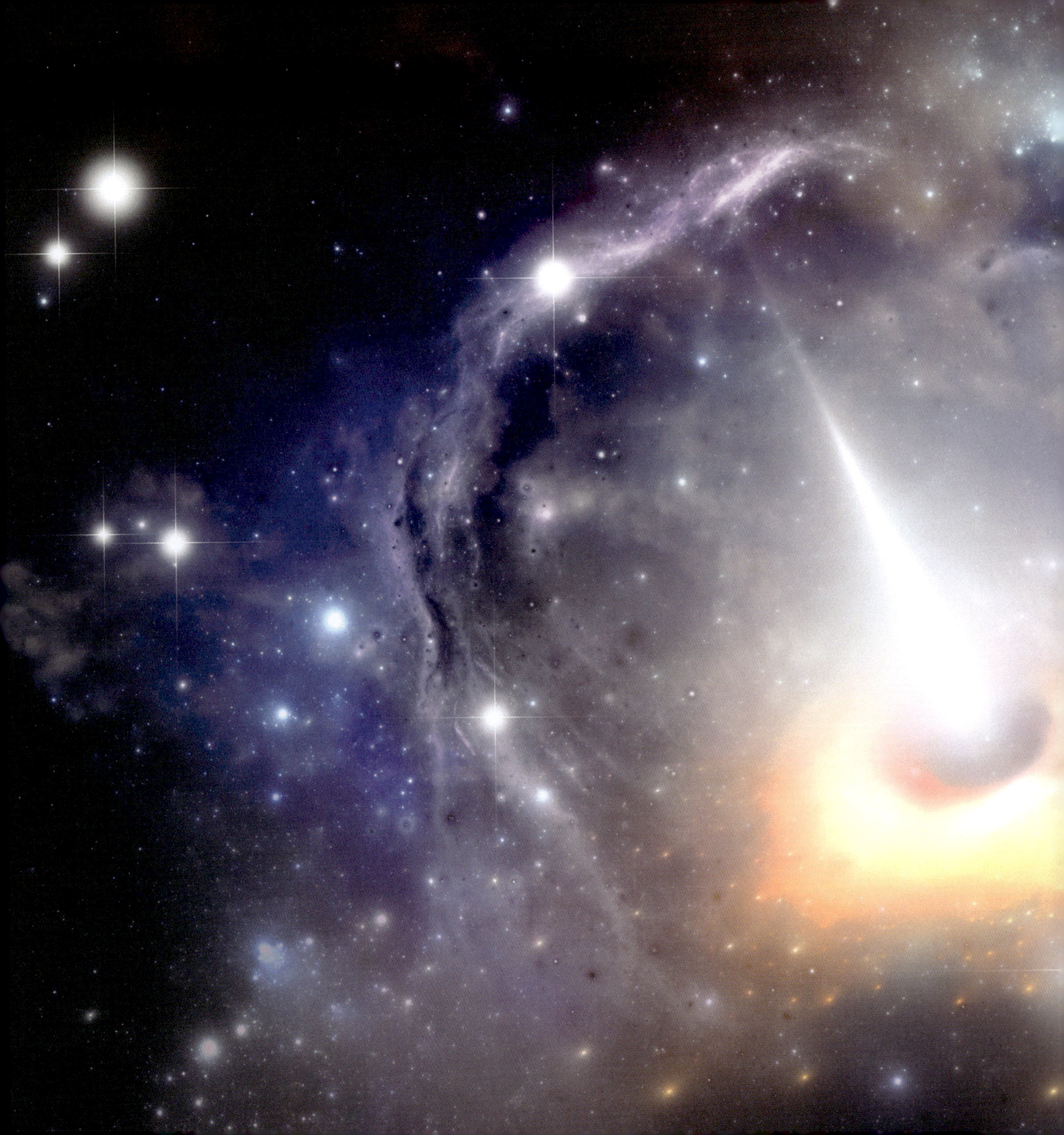

Some scientists studied and researched the Big Bang Theory. They came up with the idea that the Big Bang was the reason why space and time were created.

It is believed that a large amount of energy was released into and pushed the tiny point into an expanding space, the universe, when the Bang happened. The universe gets bigger and bigger, like a balloon filling with air. It started to make more space.

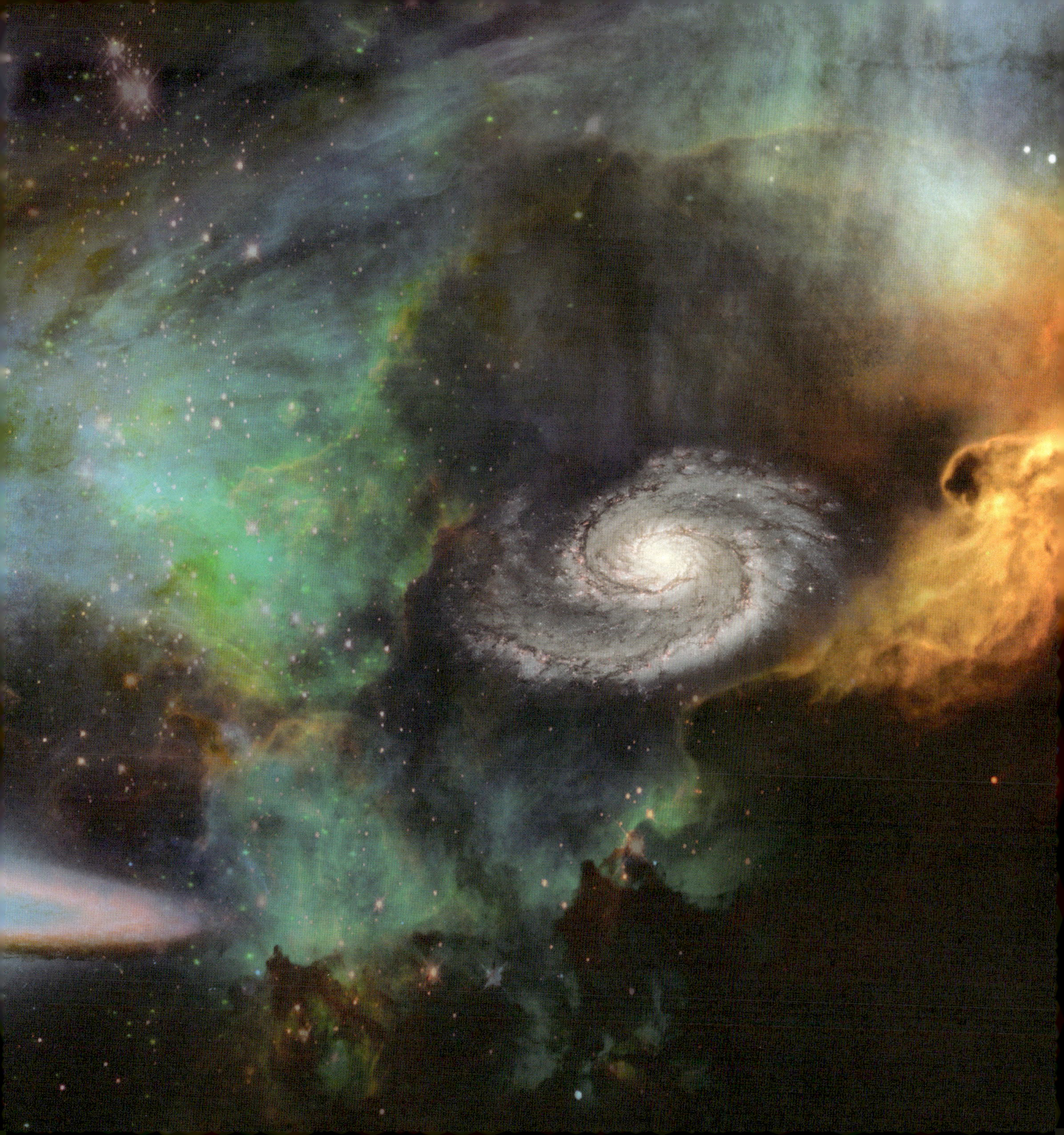

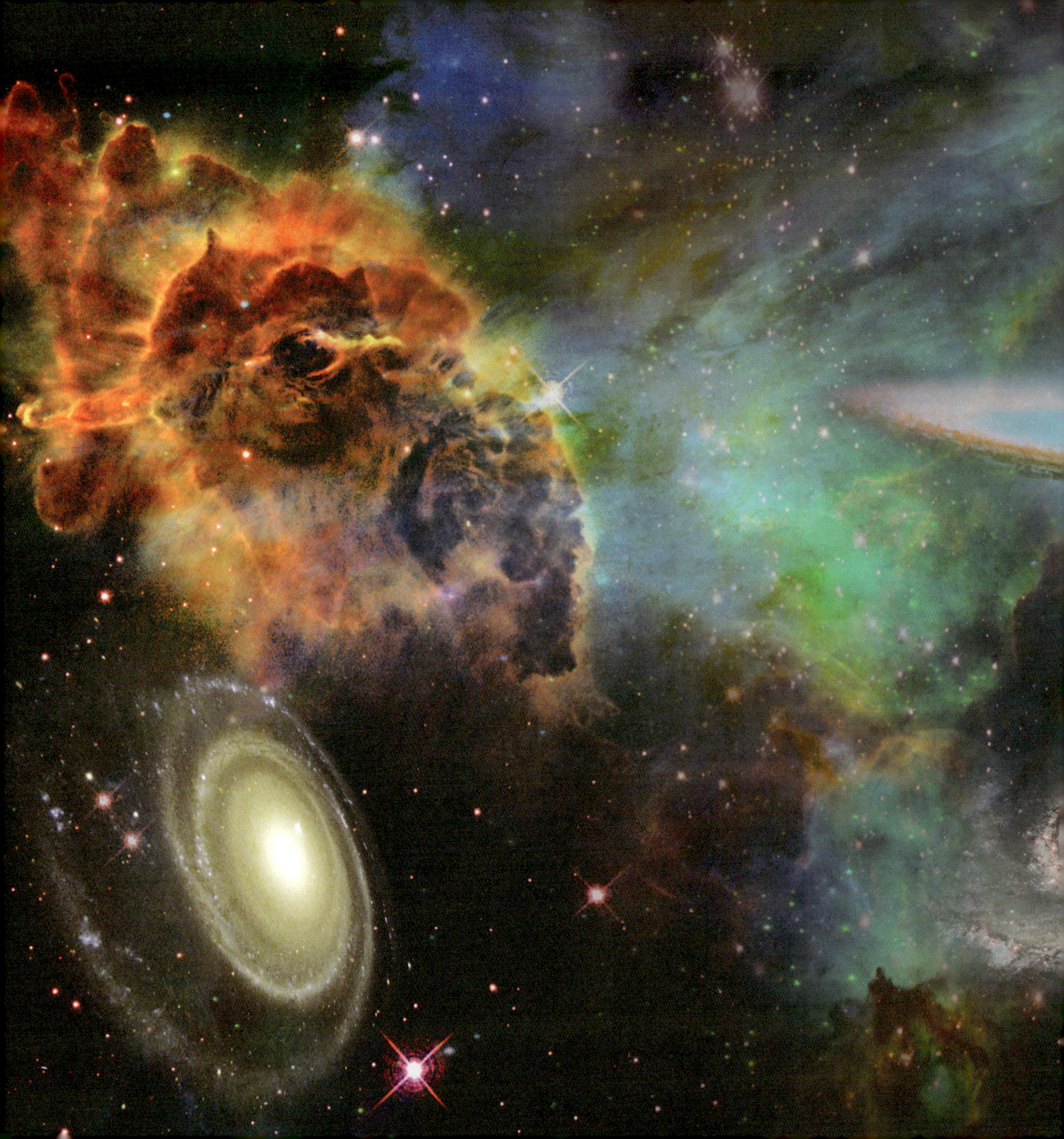

In the 1920's, Edwin Hubble, an astronomer, developed a theory that the universe is not static. He believed that the universe is expanding and contracting continuously. The universe is believed to have no end. Its limits curve, so you never reach a wall or a cliff.

What came out when the universe started to expand?

As the temperature dropped below 1 billion degrees Celsius, protons and neutrons came together. . These atoms became nebulae which developed into stars. A nebula is a gigantic cloud of dust and gas.

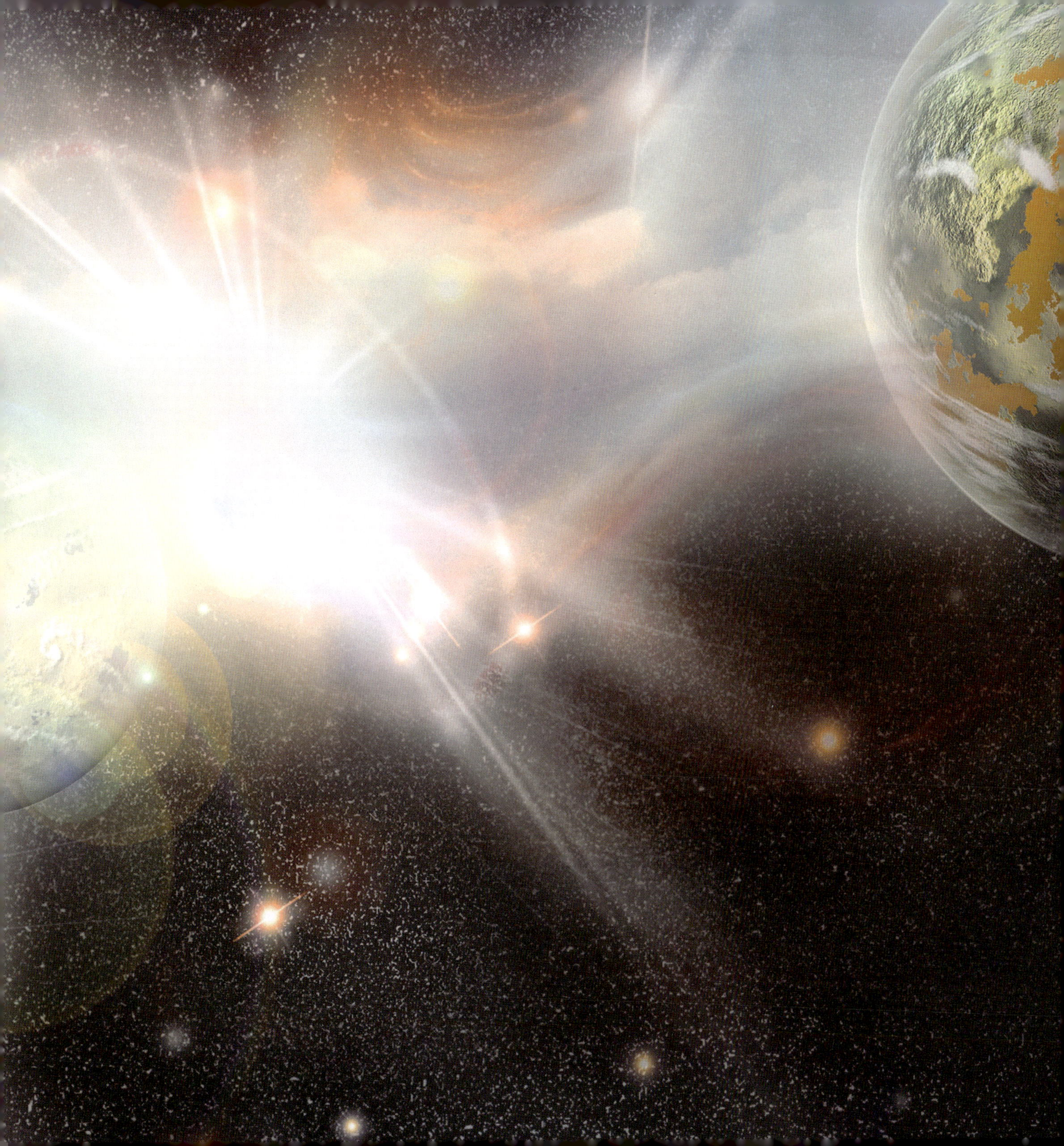

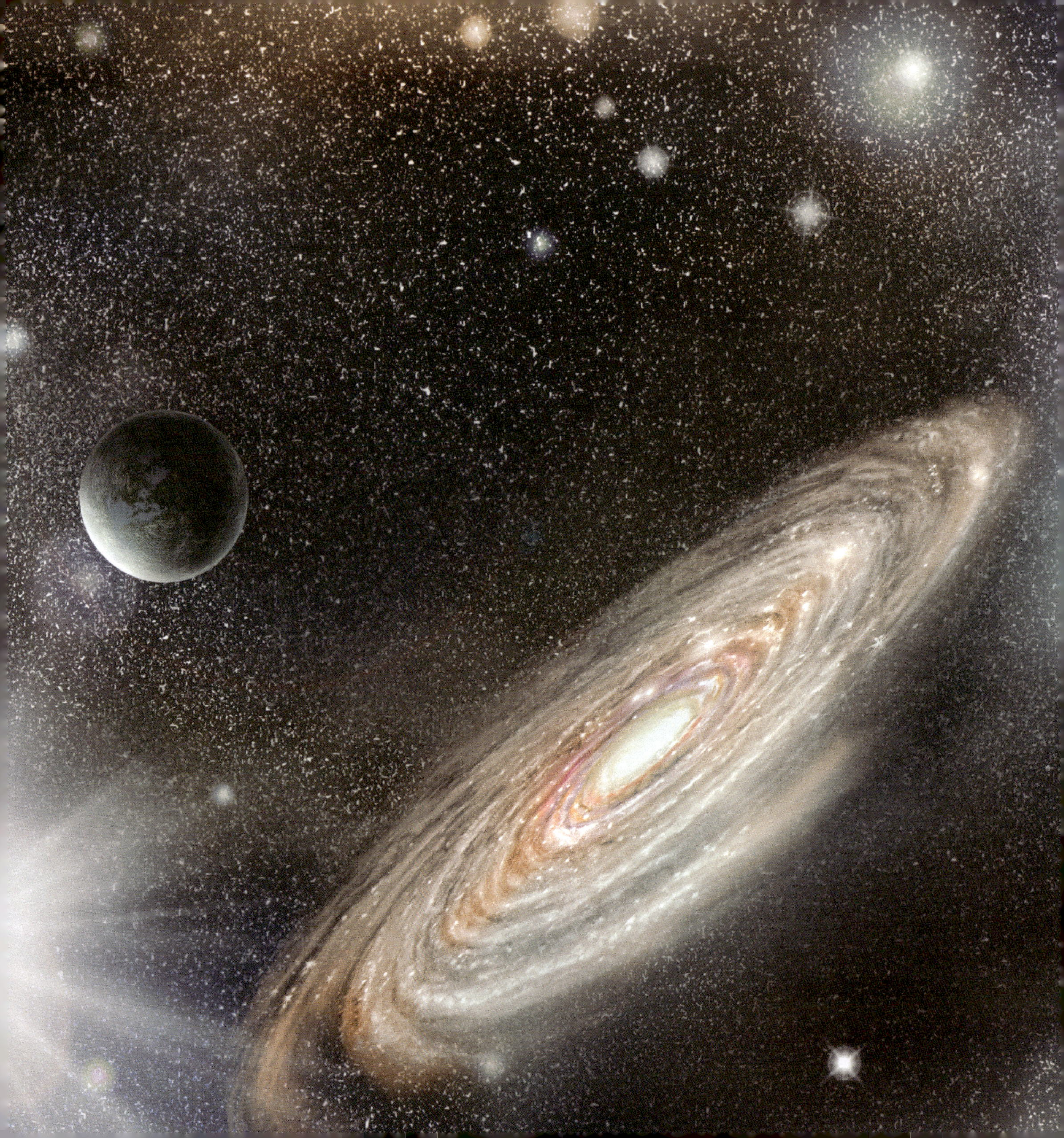

As the dust and gas in the nebulae contract the clouds get hotter and denser. As the clouds get dense, they become hot enough to ignite their hydrogen fuel. It begins its new life as a star! That is why a nebula is referred to as a star factory.

Once atoms began to gather into objects, gravity came into existence. Gravity is the force of attraction between objects.

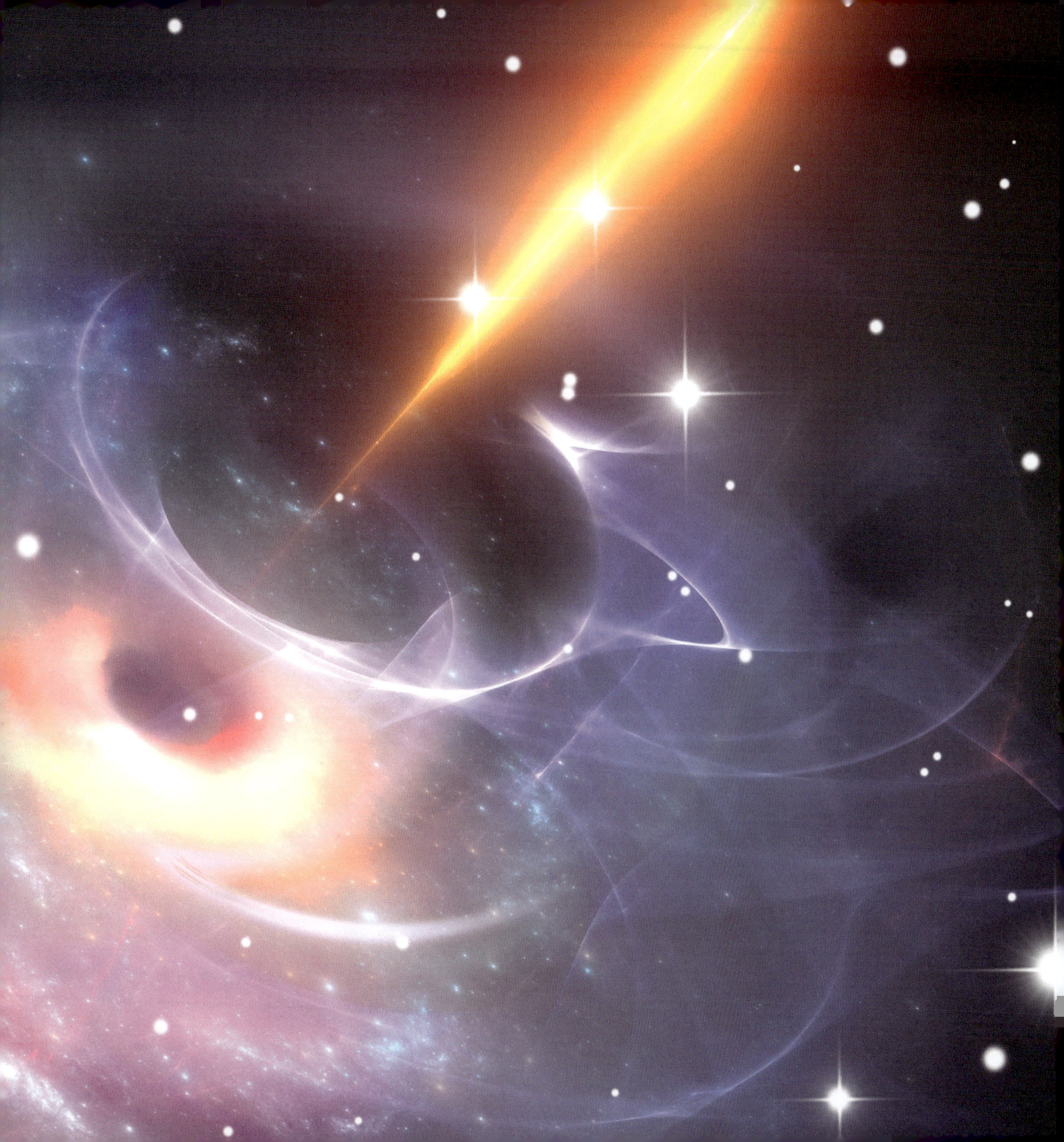

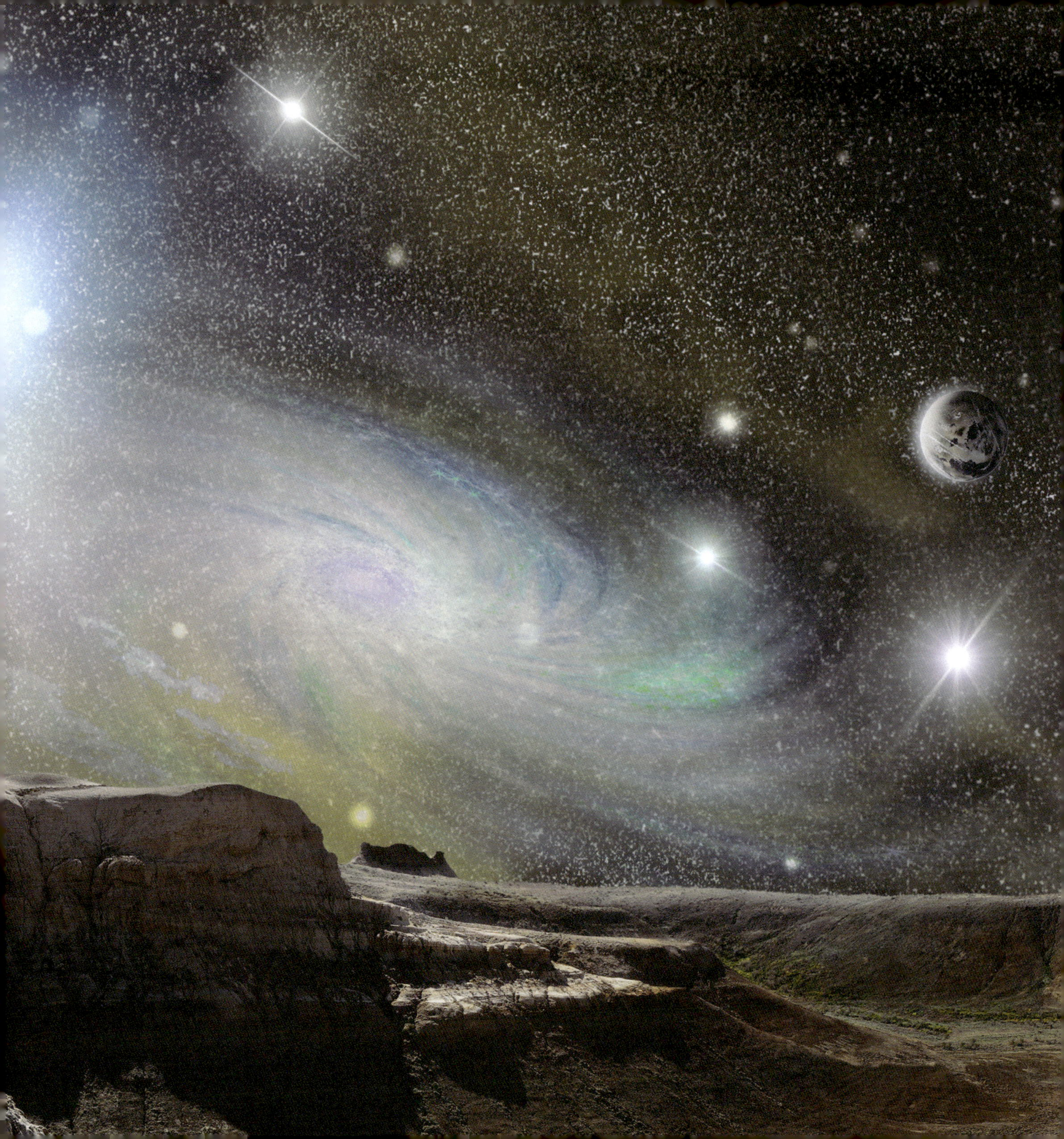

What makes the Universe expand?

It may be that the universe accelerates at a huge rate because of dark energy. It may be that the universe accelerates at a huge rate because of dark energy.

Only 4% of the things in the universe can be seen. These include the galaxies, planets and stars. The remaining 96% of the things in the universe are dark matter or dark energy, and can't be seen.

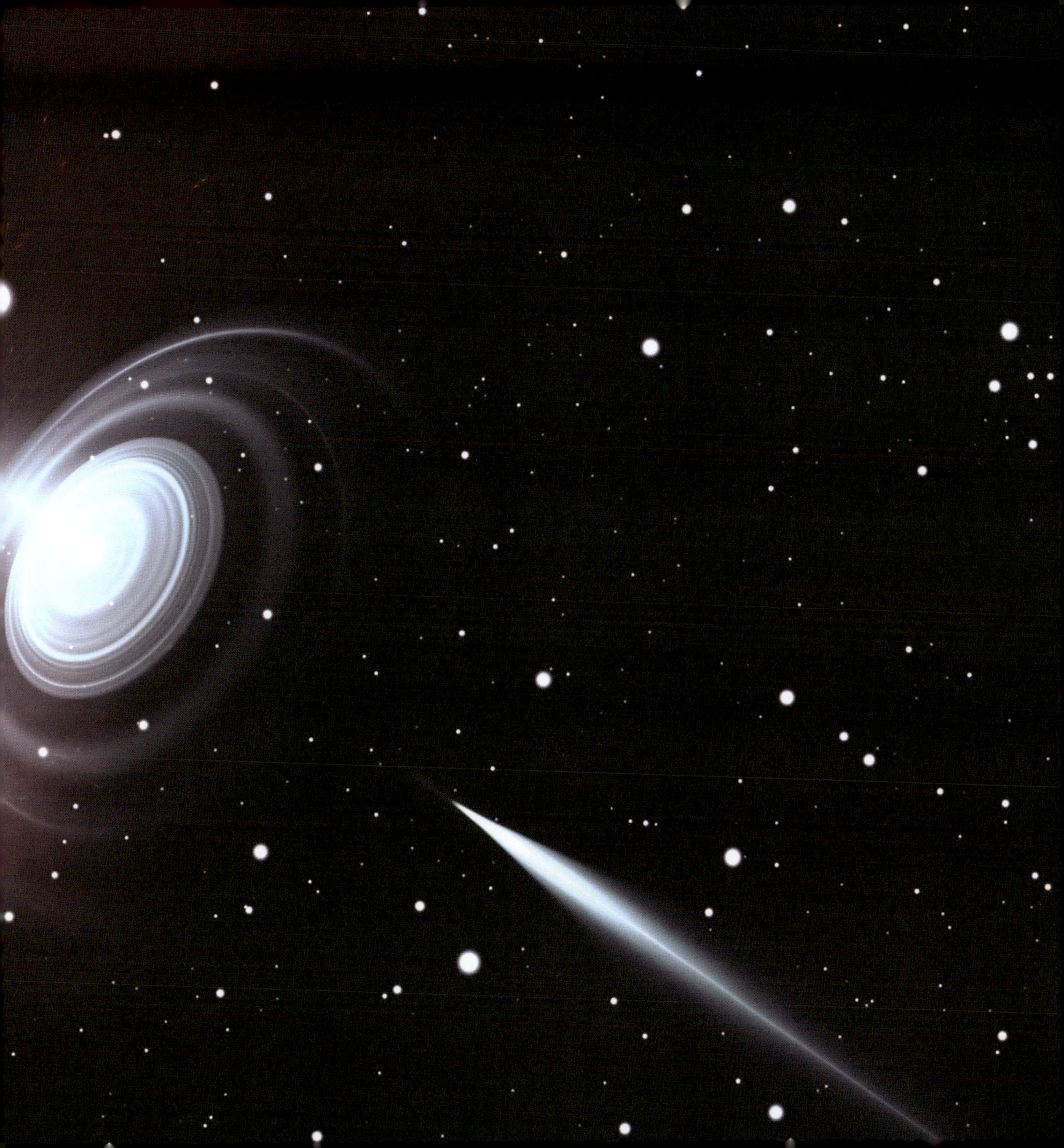

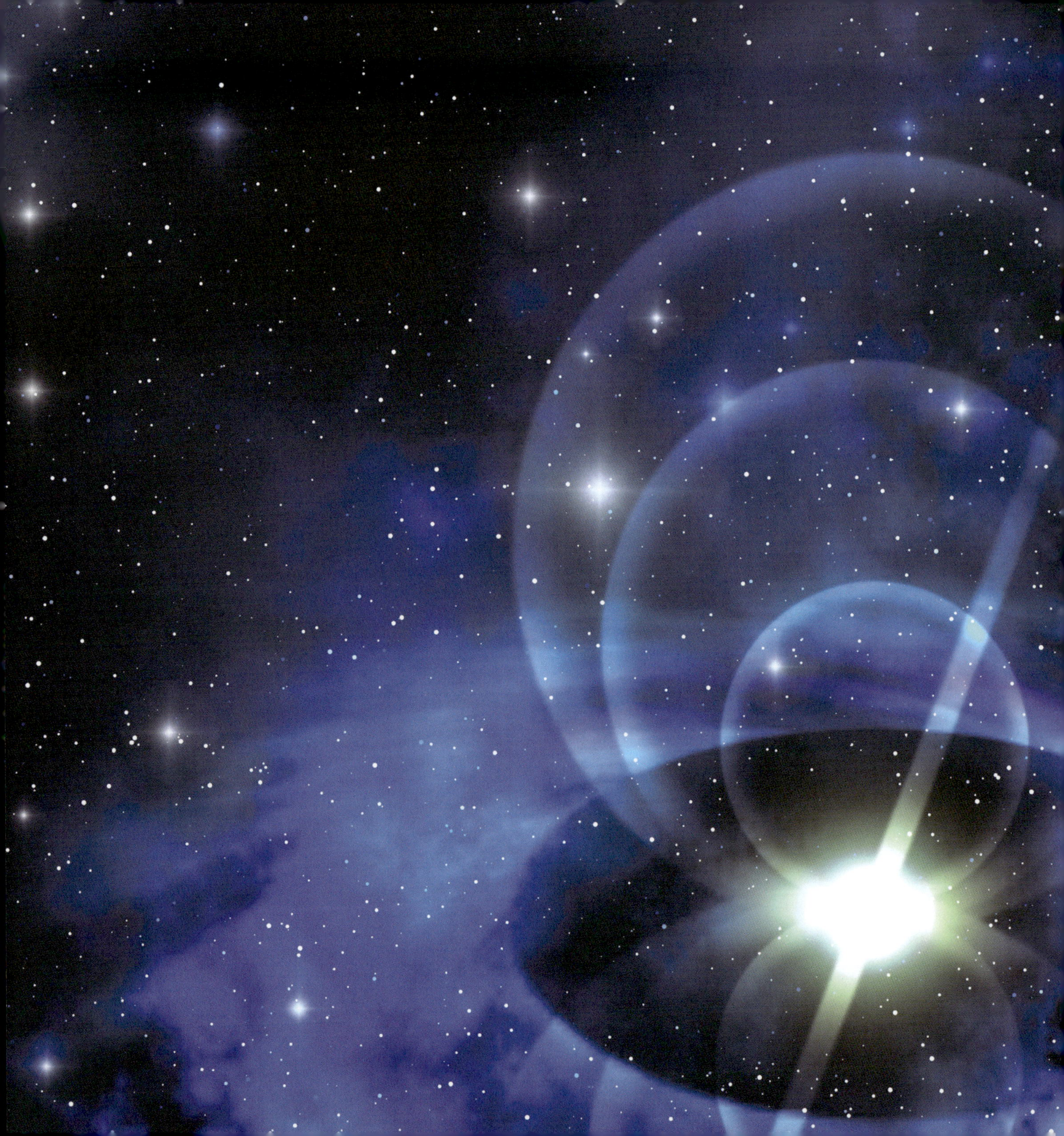

It is believed that the Universe continues to expand to this day. We are in it. We are the incredible creatures living on our unique planet, Earth. It's unique because it's the only planet we know of so far that contains and sustains life.

This is the amazing Big Bang! The big explosion of the tiny point or bubble started it all.

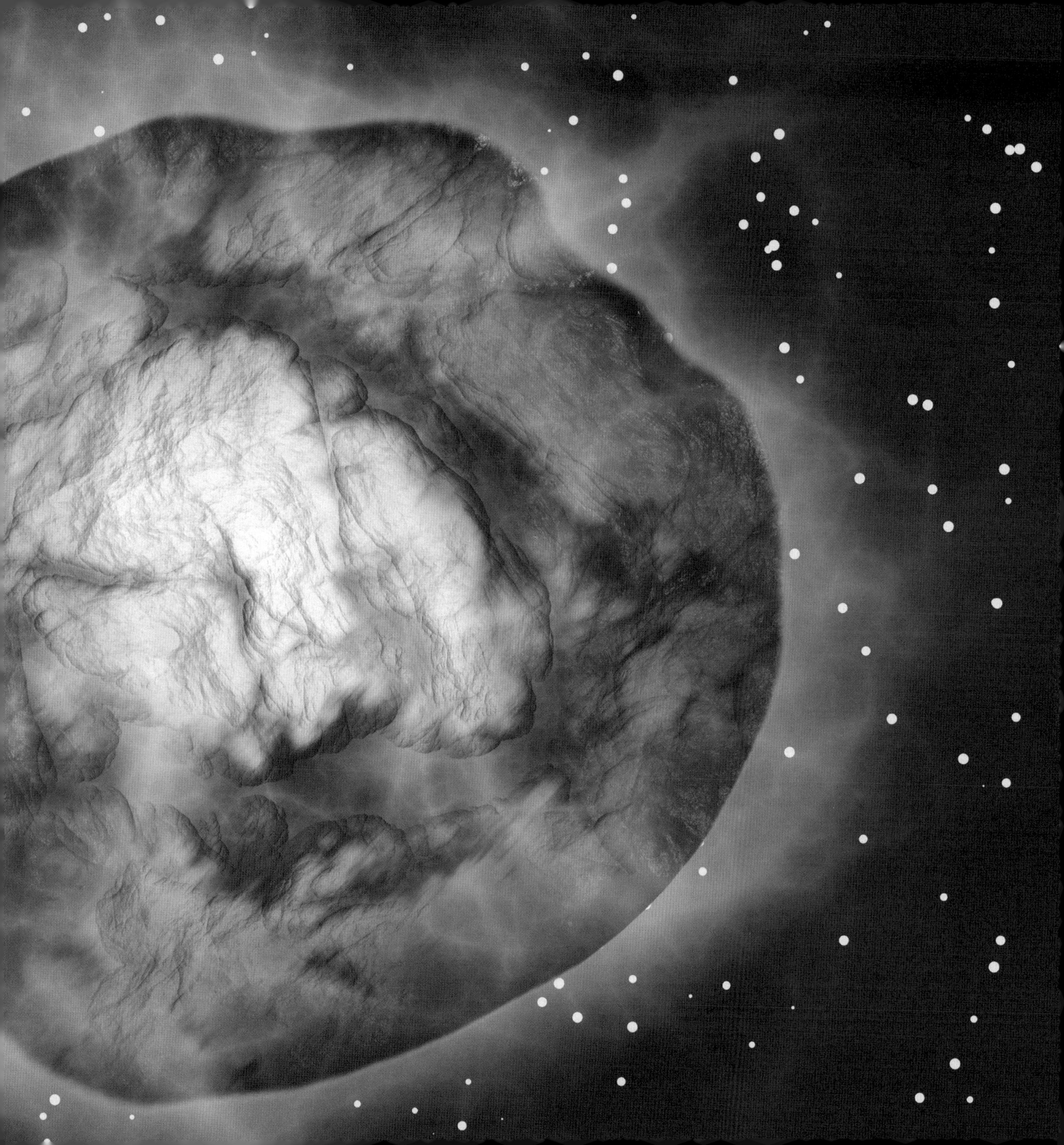

Printed in Great Britain
by Amazon